COLD, SOFT, TENDER

An Erotic Horror Short

ANNABETH LEONG

Created with Vellum

PRAISE FOR ANNABETH LEONG

Annabeth Leong is a mistress of the bittersweet fantasy with the unpredictable conclusion.

— JEAN ROBERTA, AUTHOR OF *SEX IS ALL METAPHORS*

Let's face it, this author is firmly in charge of her pen. She takes imaginative risks that really pay off. She understands the true depths and creativity of sexual connection… including the pain and euphoria it can bring. She tunes deeply into the human spirit and the myths that lie buried in us all. She knows how we struggle and isn't afraid of emotions. She has a very big heart and her imagination is boundless.

— LANA FOX, CO-FOUNDER, GO DEEPER PRESS

I'll eagerly read anything by Annabeth Leong.

— LISABET SARAI, AUTHOR OF THE TOYMAKERS GUILD BOOKS

I

2014 A.D., in a barrow near Egtved, Denmark

Lauren Patterson packed up the last of the archeological team's tools. She'd grown used to the earthy stench of the ancient gravesite, and she'd learned to trust the sturdiness of its construction, so the fear and wonder she'd felt the first time she'd entered that place had long faded. At the moment, she was simply irritated.

The rest of the team had gone off to get beers. She had an invitation to join them, but as the most junior member, she had a lot of cleanup to get through before she would feel free to screw off the way she wanted to.

It wasn't just the need for beer and socializing getting to her. There was also the matter of Tore. She'd moved to Denmark to be with that tall, blond bastard, giving up her preferred concentration on South American cultures. She was lucky to have this job, she knew, lucky to be working in her chosen field at all, but there were days when the cold, rainy Danish weather made her feel bitter, when she thought about the years of Spanish language study she'd wasted, the questions her thesis had raised that she'd dreamed of one day answering.

She closed a plastic box much harder than necessary. A crack appeared around the latch, and Lauren cursed under her breath. The barrow made her words echo oddly, returning them to her in the voice of a stranger.

Lauren shook her head and tried to summon a positive attitude.

This project on women from the Bronze Age was a significant one. Her colleagues were friendly. Hell, they all spoke great English, so it sometimes barely seemed to matter that she'd moved to a foreign country.

Except when it mattered. Like when Tore went on long business trips and Lauren was forced to realize she had no real friends in this place. Like when she tried to hang out with her team and realized that when they got drunk they made all their jokes in Danish.

Here she was, staring down the barrel of another lonely weekend. She knew this was a grand adventure. She wanted to be brave, to explore historical castles and try traditional varieties of smørrebrød and climb to the top of Rådhustårnet. She didn't feel brave this afternoon, though. She wanted to lie on the couch with her boyfriend's arms around her and feel loved.

Not that Tore would be into that sort of thing. No matter how many times she asked him not to leave hickeys on her, he couldn't seem to keep his teeth away from her neck. He laughed, did what he wanted, and offered to buy her turtleneck sweaters. And she didn't seem able to put up any true resistance. She remembered a time when she had stood up for herself readily, with lovers and everyone else, but that will had somehow been sapped in recent years.

This was probably the reason she hadn't gotten to South

America. When a real chance presented itself, she'd been afraid, and had followed Tore instead.

What did that say about her? She cursed again and glanced toward the direction where Egtvedpigen had been found. That body was one of the most famous Bronze Age remnants in Denmark, if not the world. All sorts of mystery surrounded it—what was with the woman's ceremonial attire? The offering of beer at her feet? The ashes of a child's bones that had been buried with her?

The team she now worked for had solved one major part of the puzzle, however, not long before Lauren joined them, and to Lauren's mind it came as a pathetic wakeup call. Egtvedpigen, the girl from Egtved, had come from far away, probably somewhere in Germany, probably as part of an arranged marriage or trade for Danish amber. Her child had died in transit, and she'd died not long after her arrival near what was now Egtved.

In other words, Egtvedpigen had followed a man to Denmark and found only death and despair along the way.

Lauren knew her boss saw things differently. Egtvedpigen's journeys meant more possibilities for Bronze Age women than had previously been thought. They could travel.

They could die far from home.

Lauren sighed, the breath scraping in her lungs like bone scraping over stone. Not for the first time, she considered what would happen if she broke up with Tore. Was it too late to look for positions in South America after all? Her life was moving both faster and slower than she wanted it to.

It felt noisy in the barrow. She'd learned a long time ago that such places were never truly silent. There were air currents that whistled and shrieked, the sounds of earth settling, and the surprisingly loud noises she made herself as she moved in the confined space. Still, she could have sworn she'd heard someone moving. Maybe one of the other team members had taken pity on her?

"Lars?" she called. He was kind. If someone had come back to help her, it seemed likely to be him.

No response came in words, but the noise was getting closer. More sounds, and the rustling of animal hides, and the intoxicating and pungent scent of strong Danish beer. It had to be someone from the team, drunk already—the movements sounded unsteady, and the low corridors and crawl spaces in the barrow weren't easy to navigate even when sober. Maybe it wasn't Lars, and maybe whoever it was hadn't heard her voice or didn't feel like responding to English.

"*Hej?*" Lauren called, her halting Danish making her questioning tone much sharper than it had to be. "*Hvem er det? Er der nogen?*" Her grammar was probably wrong, but whoever it was should get the point. She wanted to know if someone was there.

Lauren stood as straight as the barrow allowed—she wasn't tall herself, but people had been much shorter in the Bronze Age than they were now, so her shoulders hunched uncomfortably. Her head spun, as if she'd been the one out drinking, and the fermented scent seemed to fill the chamber entirely, choking out the oxygen.

A moment later, a woman appeared in the entryway, her movements jerky. She finished crawling and stood, brushing barrow dust off bare brown knees. She wore a short skirt made of leather tassels, a fur capelet around her shoulders, a necklace of improbably large amber beads, and a large round belt buckle the dark color of heavily tarnished bronze. Her hair was brown and coarse, held back by a comb that appeared to be made of animal horn. She was short and small and seemed only just old enough to drink in a bar, but the gaze she fixed on Lauren was ancient and knowing, and the set of her jaw was proud and regal.

She looked for all the world like a computer rendering of Egtvedpigen, and Lauren laughed out loud at what had to be a practical joke.

The woman frowned and stepped closer, and Lauren closed her mouth, suddenly uncertain.

2

1370 B.C., Farther North Than She Dreamed Possible

She was not the first woman he had brought to this place, nor the first to come from a faraway village, nor the first to sicken under his ministrations. The sight of the neat row of burial mounds behind his home should perhaps have horrified her, but she had felt very little since the first night he had come to her.

His touch had not been cruel, not as the word was commonly understood. In fact, she had spread her legs for him willingly, both because she knew what was expected of her and because she liked his height and the eerie lightness of his eyes. He had surprised her by exploring her with his hands before he took her—the men she had been with before had not bothered with such niceties.

She had closed her eyes and soaked in the touch, willing to forgive the chill of his skin in light of the fire it woke along her inner thighs.

He began with her face, cupping her cheek, then her chin, then running a finger along her lower lip. He opened all her clothes, though that wasn't necessary for what she'd thought was his purpose, then stared at her naked body until she shivered under the gaze. Slowly, he ran the backs of his hands from her shoulders to her wrists, along her sides, over her hips, and down the tops of her thighs.

He rested a palm on her breast as if testing its softness, then caressed her nipple with a thumb.

Her teeth began to chatter. When a man took her fast, a wildness awoke in her and brought strength to her spine. She felt powerful like an animal, meeting his thrusts, howling agony and ecstasy into the night.

This way of touching, though—it made her feel weak and a little frightened. She had not known what would happen to her when this man took her from her village and her home, and she had tried to think of neither future nor past during the long, arduous journey. In this moment, he left her no choice but to think, to wonder about where she had been and where she was going. It felt as if he could shape her like so much river clay, turn her into a vessel from which he could drink. Her fingers trembled, and then her legs.

Still, his soft touch continued, plucking her nipple as if testing a blade. He lowered his lips to her breast. She whimpered, and the next time he brought his thumb to her nipple, her body met his with a tight, sharp point.

He hummed satisfaction and returned his mouth to her as his hands shifted lower.

Her belly quivered under his fingertips. What she felt was fear, except that her thighs spread wider of their own volition. She anticipated pain, but she arched toward it, toward him. She wanted to get this over with, except that the way his body traveled hers made her ache with an odd mixture of longing and revulsion.

She wished they shared more language, but they communicated mostly through grunts and gestures, and she had no idea how to express her complicated feelings in such a crude way. That added to her fear, now that she had no choice but to think about it. It was utterly different to be in this position with a man she couldn't talk to—not at all like being with the men from her own village.

She whimpered again, this time unprovoked by a touch, and he seemed to take the sound as encouragement.

She was wet to the tops of her thighs. There was no denying that she was affected by the strangeness of this, by her fear, by her vulnerability to a man she didn't know. He made a sound she couldn't interpret when he found her sticky fluids, and brought damp fingers to her lips as if she somehow needed him to introduce her to herself.

Anger flashed through her, but she parted her lips for her own pungent flavor.

His forehead came to rest against hers, and now he cast aside his clothing and brought his member between her legs. He probed her slit bluntly, without finesse, but she was so wet that her body guided him into her easily. She was a river that could not help but lead him to its source, and she gasped sharply as he entered her.

Now came the wildness. Her hips pushed up, and she moved to grind her pelvis against his.

He stilled within her and pressed her down with strong, cold fingers. She didn't understand and cocked her head to one side in question. His hands grew firmer, holding her in place.

He withdrew more slowly than she had ever felt before, then reentered her with equal deliberation. The nature of the motion made him feel huge within her, overwhelming. She cried out and tried to buck upward, and he pushed her down again.

He murmured a few words she didn't recognize, and his hands moved over her, pressing her thighs into the earth, her torso, her shoulders, and finally, her head. Bewildered, she lay still for a moment, and he resumed fucking her.

The teeth-chattering and trembling took her body with a vengeance, and she *had* to move against him. The moment she tried, he stopped again, looking stern and a little angry.

She whimpered, her odd mixture of fear and arousal reaching acute levels, making her belly flutter and her body ripple around his invading member. He seemed not to want her to do what came naturally. He seemed to want her to behave as if she did not feel, and yet everything he did made her feel more intensely than ever.

A tear rolled down one cheek, and it confused her even more. He was not hurting her. This mating felt better, in many ways, than any she had experienced before. And yet her chest was tight and she felt on the verge of choking.

He caught the tear with his tongue and she shuddered violently. The idea of him drinking her confusion and being pleased by it made more tears flow, and he licked them all up as he fucked her slowly.

She was still now except for the shaking she couldn't control. His every thrust sent intense feelings shooting down her legs or arcing up through her lungs. Her breath was ragged. To her own mind, she sounded timid. The bold woman she been before he removed her from her home seemed not to exist anymore.

He murmured continuously as he drank her tears. He sounded as if he was encouraging her toward something, but she didn't know what. All she could do was open wider, surrender more fully, lie still while he used her in this strange way. It was as if he wished to forbid her participation in her own body and her own feelings.

Because she had this thought, when she began to come, the pleasure was accompanied by a burst of fear. She lay as if pinned in place by his member, holding her breath because she did not know what the consequences would be for her ecstasy, or for revealing it. She tensed her muscles as hard as she could so her hips did not buck and her body did not roll toward him. As a result, her cries built inside her lungs, pressing against the inside of her ribcage. Her sensations shot into her spine and stuck there. This orgasm released things that had nowhere to flow. She felt full, in danger of bursting, apprehensive about what would happen if she did.

Her face screwed up of its own accord. She panted once, the harsh desperation of the sound reminding her of childbirth.

There was a pleased laugh against her throat, then a sharp sensation at the root of it. He had taught her to lie still for penetration, and so she did not fight or even fidget when his fangs stretched into her veins.

Everything that had gathered within her—the noise, the pleasure, the confusion, the fear, the pain—flowed out now through the holes his teeth made, along with her blood. It should have been horrifying, but instead it brought her relief. He'd made her unable to contain her own self, and now he was siphoning off some of that force, enough of her fury that she knew she would fit inside herself again after this.

She groaned. Her sex rippled around his, in time with her pulse. She felt herself becoming lighter, becoming less. It was not a sensation she would have recognized as pleasure before this night, but now she welcomed it like a sigh of air within a hot, closed place.

She let him take her, and it was soft, not wild; tender, not cruel. Life, however, was wild and cruel, and so this strange man brought her closer than she had ever been to the soft tenderness of death.

She bled into his mouth. He spent between her legs. She knew without having to wonder that he had not planted a child in her womb. Nothing could be born of the act they had shared.

When he withdrew—his teeth leaving her, his member leaving her—she was very cold. He wrapped her in furs and brought her water to drink, but those small favors did not change much. He came to her once every few nights, and it was not long before warmth was nothing more than a strange memory to her. She could recall it in only the vaguest terms, and now could not imagine what it would actually be like.

She no longer cried when he came to her, and she sensed that this disappointed him. There was so little in her now, however, that there was nothing to spill over.

Her child died somewhere along the way. She had feared the cause, and had looked carefully around the dead boy's neck for the marks of teeth. Finding none, she felt an odd sort of relief, then nothing else. She still reached sometimes, afterward, for the tiny hand that had so often clung to hers, but when it was not there, a part of her gave thanks for the ordinary sickness that had spared her son from her own chilly destiny.

It was hard for her to say what had diminished her so much. The drinking of her blood, certainly, and the nights of restraining the wild, joyful self she had once known. But that all mingled with the other hardships of the journey. Sometimes the change seemed inevitable—perhaps this numbness was simply a consequence of being so far from home, a thing all travelers must endure. Perhaps distance was the reason for this strange man's chill. Indeed, the farther north they got, the more he seemed to come to life. His cheeks grew rosier, and sometimes there was a fire in his fingertips that resembled the sun she had once known—a sun that, more often than not, hid now behind a veil of clouds.

And so she saw the burial mounds, and knew she was neither the first nor the last for him, and she recalled the sensation of her hips pressed toward the dirt as she accepted him. It all seemed natural to her now. She had softened so much inside that she saw no point in fighting anything, nor even rising to meet it.

She would have met the same end as all the others had it not been for the growling wind that echoed from the barrow mouth closest to her bedroll, for the sound of words spoken in another language she did not know, something yet more unfamiliar than the sounds of the strange man who had brought her here.

She rose from where she slept, still drunk from the evening meal, and wandered toward the sound.

❧ 3 ❧

2014 A.D.

Lauren wanted to run, but there could be no running in this place. She wanted to believe she was imagining this, but no matter how dizzy she felt, she knew there was no chemical cause for the vision she was seeing.

The woman was sick, that was obvious now. She moved in the daze of someone who had been weak for so long she'd forgotten what it was to be hale. Lauren stepped back uneasily and tried speaking again. "Hello? *Hej?*" In desperation, she added, "*Hola?*"

The woman only shook her head. She reached for Lauren's wrist, and when she caught it, her fingers tightened with shocking strength.

☙ 4 ❧

A Time Between Two Times, A Place Between Life and Death

This was another of his women, then, still living, though perhaps not for long. She took in the strange garments of the woman before her, and the even stranger colors of her hair and skin. As unfamiliar as the woman was on the outside, though, it was easy to recognize that look in her eyes. She was lost, far from home, and cold where she used to be warm. She was learning to take softly what she might once have met wildly.

The woman made incomprehensible sounds. She had not yet realized many of the truths of her situation—that much was clear.

Though they could not speak, a touch could tell the story. She grabbed the woman's wrist and did not let go.

5

Not Drunk, Definitely Unmoored from Reality

This was no prank. Lauren could feel that in the otherworldly grip around her wrist. She got the idea—as unhinged as it was—that the woman before her would answer to no modern language. Random, useless facts ran through her mind. She'd taken some courses that alluded to current scholarly thoughts on the proto-Germanic languages, but no one really knew how they would have sounded, and Lauren couldn't remember what little she'd learned of the words current academics guessed might have been used.

She was trapped in a world of disconnection, but at the moment that did not feel so different from the rest of her life. In some ways, the touch of this strange woman spoke more eloquently than Tore's long, one-sided Skype conversations, and certainly more than the utilitarian discussions she shared with her fellow scientists.

There was real desperation in this touch, along with a sense of understanding and being understood.

Without meaning to, Lauren let out a whimper, and her counterpart comprehended this wordless sound entirely. She stepped close enough for Lauren to smell the beer on her breath and the ancient earth in her hair.

Gently, the woman tugged at the collar of Lauren's turtleneck sweater, revealing the base of her neck, brushing fingertips over it and squinting. Lauren didn't know what she was looking for, but her fingers were soft and strong.

A few moments into the examination, she sucked in a breath as the woman dug into a bruise Tore had left the last time they'd made love. It hurt more than Lauren expected. Hickeys were not really *that* big a deal, Tore had told her plenty of times. She'd gotten used to having them in the years they'd been together. It shocked her to see dull red colors behind her eyes as the woman explored the tender spot.

She placed her hand over the woman's fingers and gently pulled them away.

The Bronze Age woman's eyes softened. She tilted her head and guided Lauren's hand to a spot previously hidden by hair and shadow, where a wholly similar bruise discolored her flesh. Lauren leaned closer, unnerved.

The reason for Egtvedpigen's death was unknown. According to everything modern science could reveal, she'd been young and healthy. She had good teeth. Her remains bore no signs of common illnesses from the time.

The mark they shared seemed significant, but Lauren shied away from the connections her brain wanted to make. Tore had given Lauren a hickey, and it was only an odd coincidence that this other woman also had one. Maybe there was some hallucinatory chemical in the barrow's air—never mind that the team had been working there without incident for years.

There had to be a logical explanation for what Lauren was experiencing. Lauren was letting herself think of this woman as Egtvedpigen, but Egtvedpigen had died more than a thousand years before the birth of Christ. She had died before the existence of modern language, before any European discovery of North America. Hell, she had died before people learned how to forge tools of iron. There was no way she stood before Lauren now, much less that a hickey could reveal the answer to the unsolved mystery of her death.

There was absolutely no chance that Lauren herself carried any connection to that death. After all, she wasn't dying—no matter that she might sometimes feel as if she were.

Still, she peered at the mark on the woman's neck, and she stiffened when she felt two clear puncture marks under her fingertips, the scabs over them hidden by the general discoloration of the bruise. She jerked to standing as if pulled by strings and touched her own hickey for the first time. She had never examined it closely—she had always felt an aversion to looking at the marks Tore left on her.

There, sure as her own breath, she found two puncture wounds, perfectly matching those on the neck of Egtvedpigen.

Lauren met the other woman's eyes, aware that she was several steps behind in understanding. There was no impatience in her companion's gaze, only compassion.

Lauren thought of Tore, and her head crowded with ridiculous folklore. Had he ever objected to garlic? Had she seen him outside in the day? Surely, she had. She would remember if he'd ever acted strangely.

None of those details mattered, though. As a scientist, she knew that, while folklore often related to the historical and scientific considerations of a culture, it rarely matched them perfectly. What mattered was the hard evidence—in this case, the puncture wounds.

Yet she resisted forming the name of the supernatural creature in her mind. It felt too farfetched and silly.

When she reached toward the woman in front of her, she

felt flesh the same temperature as her own, as solid as her own. If Egtvedpigen did not stand before her, and if Tore was not after all a vampire, then Lauren had well and truly lost her mind.

Egtvedpigen's fingers intertwined with hers and squeezed hard. Lauren sank to the floor alongside her, overwhelmed by the thoughts swirling through her head. She often felt weak after she and Tore made love, even dizzy. She often got terrible headaches. She'd looked that all up online, though. It wasn't uncommon for women to get headaches after strong orgasms—and her orgasms with Tore were certainly among the strongest she'd had.

Blood loss, though... That would explain more than she cared to admit. She thought about how heavily she'd slept after the last time, and how she'd woken up groggy and feeling hungover, though it had been several days since she'd last had a drink.

She glanced at the woman beside her. "You know, don't you?" Lauren said aloud. "You aren't questioning yourself. You don't look like the type to question much of anything." Back in the Bronze Age, when a man could claim a woman in exchange for a nice hunk of amber, there probably wasn't much to stop him from capturing a woman as bold and fierce as Egtvedpigen seemed. Now, in modern times, if a man were a vampire, he'd have to do a little more. He'd have to make the woman think it was her own idea to follow him. He'd have to make her love him, and he'd have to convince her that he returned the feeling.

She thought of the sense she got when she and Tore talked on Skype—that she was an annoyance, that he murmured endearments without feeling, and that he resented listening to what she had to say. In person, that all melted away beside his obvious need for her body, the passion that inspired him to leave hickeys on her neck even when she asked him not to. Lauren had told herself that Tore was simply more comfortable expressing his feelings physically than verbally, but now she saw potential for a different motive.

The woman beside Lauren spoke, too, and her words were as strange as expected. They came from a lost time, as difficult to decode as the silent bones around them in the barrow, and they would not easily divulge their secrets.

Lauren stared into Egtvedpigen's eyes, her throat tight with longing. This woman understood things that Lauren had never been able to describe, not even to herself. Maybe she felt the same about Lauren. Yet they were divided from each other, and Lauren had no idea of how to bridge the gap, no matter how desperately she wanted to.

The sudden sensation of the woman's lips against hers made her jerk away. Lauren had never kissed another woman before and hadn't expected to start now. Her face felt as if it were on fire. Slowly, she forced herself to return to meeting Egtvedpigen's gaze.

There was frustration in the Bronze Age woman's expression, and Lauren thought she understood why. There was more than one way to communicate, and if words weren't possible... She took a deep breath and lifted a hand to Egtvedpigen's cheek.

Her skin was soft when Lauren stroked it, but the other woman flinched from her touch. She pushed Lauren's hand away and grabbed Lauren's shoulder instead, her hands ungentle, her fingers like claws.

Lauren wasn't sure what Egtvedpigen wanted, and she wasn't sure what she wanted herself. She held still and waited to see what would happen.

Egtvedpigen moved to kiss her again. Everything Lauren had ever heard about the softness of a woman's touch seemed like a lie in that moment. This was a kiss of fire and anger, laced with the heady, hoppy flavor of ancient beer. It warmed her more than any food or blanket or heater had in years. It felt good, in a strange way, but as soon as Lauren began to melt for it, the other woman backed away, her frustration even more prominent.

Egtvedpigen took Lauren's hand and lifted it. She mimed the grabbing motion she'd used herself and wasn't satisfied until Lauren squeezed her hard. Testing the reaction, Lauren did the same with the other hand, and was rewarded with a sharp, approving grunt.

Was this a Bronze Age version of enthusiastic consent? Lauren didn't know what to make of the insistence on a firm grip, but when she stepped in to continue their kissing, she made sure to come in strong, and Egtvedpigen seemed to like that, parting her lips readily for Lauren and bringing her tongue forward to meet Lauren's own.

A barrow was a weird place for a makeout session, but the thought didn't stop Lauren. Kissing Egtvedpigen made her feel rough and dirty, like a wild animal of some sort—and more alive than she had in years.

She propelled the other woman toward the ground and drove her knee into the space between Egtvedpigen's thighs. Lauren felt strong, in a way that reminded her how long it had been since the last time she could say that.

Egtvedpigen's leather skirt covered little, so Lauren didn't bother to try to remove it. Instead, she reached under it and quickly discovered the life-giving heat of the other woman's cunt. It wasn't yet particularly wet, so Lauren teased it open, careful to keep her touch firm. She held Egtvedpigen's mound in her palm and squeezed until her hips rocked upward. She pressed knuckles against her entrance until it began to respond by sucking gently at her fingers. She found her clit but didn't pull back the hood to expose it. Instead, she manipulated the skin around it, more roughly than she could have done had the sensitive flesh stood bare.

It wasn't exactly what she would have liked to have done to herself, but she judged from Egtvedpigen's reactions that she wasn't far off the mark.

What mattered to Lauren was the way strength poured into her as she touched her ancient counterpart. Everything about this encounter was sharp and earthy—from the pattern of the other woman's breathing to the longing that awakened between Lauren's thighs. It felt like waking up with a shock, blinking into a bright shaft of sunlight. Lauren's thoughts moved in a way they hadn't since she'd left America. Memories came to her constantly—Tore, his grin predatory until he realized she was watching; the indulgent sound in his voice when they argued, the way they both knew Lauren would back down eventually. She let all that fade before the images in front of her now—Egtvedpigen's head thrown back, her mouth wide in a snarl of pleasure, her heels digging tracks into the dirt as she strained to meet Lauren's every gesture.

Egtvedpigen scrabbled at Lauren's clothes, but the workings of buttons and zippers seemed to escape her. Lauren released her just long enough to help and was rewarded with rough, grasping fingers pushing into her cunt.

She responded in kind, pressing inside the other woman now, rutting with her on the dirt floor of the barrow.

Egtvedpigen growled and rolled onto Lauren, driving herself onto Lauren's hand with wild abandon, her fur capelet askew, her eyes fiery, a feral grin splitting her mouth.

She was glorious. She was a match that lit the brittle kindling of Lauren's body aflame. As if possessed, Lauren arched toward her.

Tore liked her to be quiet, no matter how passionately he fucked her or how fiercely he bit at her throat. So it was a shock to hear her own voice, rising now to match Egtvedpigen's, cursing in a way that made the specific definitions of the words irrelevant.

They were united. They were alive. And as she coaxed an orgasm forward by working herself on Egtvedpigen's fingers, she knew they would be free. This pleasure, this moment, belonged to her and was shared willingly. She was not being taken or controlled. The orgasm would not be bestowed upon her as an instrument of confusion or a demonstration of power. It would be hers, won by her strength and the power of her thighs, earned by means of a primitive, never-forgotten rhythm, by the luscious rocking of hips and the firm rippling of a moistened cunt.

They were animal, and therefore human, and it had never been clearer to her that Tore was somehow not.

Above her, Egtvedpigen panted, then wailed, and there was unmistakable triumph in the sound, even as the heat and grip of her cunt became almost unbearable around Lauren's fingers.

She didn't stop moving, not even after she came. Egtvedpigen rocked as if fucking Lauren's hand was a requirement of bringing Lauren pleasure. She moved as if her entire body was a cunt and she might swallow Lauren whole, or as if her being swelled with the single-minded purpose of a cock and she would thrust until release was found.

In the face of her wildness, Lauren found herself wild, too. She felt as if she was climbing to an impossible, breathtaking height. Her ass ached from the effort of pressing up. Sweat matted dirt into her hair.

But she reached her goal. She snatched her own pleasure from the thick, heavy air.

As she did, Egtvedpigen's body became less solid. Lauren sagged back onto the dirt, a little embarrassed by her state of disarray, but sated nevertheless.

She noticed that she didn't feel sleepy after sex this time.

And after she put away the team's equipment, she didn't meet anyone for beers after all. Instead, she went home and packed her things, changed her contact information, and got online to get in touch with her old advisor and former classmates and colleagues, putting out the word that she was looking to get back into her old research focus.

Lauren wasn't sure if she could resist should Tore come to reclaim her, but she forced herself to look at the healing mark on her neck every day, and to practice in the mirror, telling him that he was no longer invited into any part of her life.

⁂ 6 ⁂

2014 A.D., in an office in Nationalmuseet in København, Denmark

"I often wonder if *she* ever missed home." Lærke Rasmussen, the principal investigator on Lauren's team, nodded toward the charts that displayed the group's findings, not directly acknowledging the letter Lauren had placed on her desk. "Egtvedkvinden certainly worked her way up to a prominent place in society, but it can't have been easy to travel so far from all she knew, especially not back then."

Egtvedkvinden. Not Egtvedpigen. The *woman* from Egtved, not the girl. Lauren was still getting used to the subtle changes in the world around her since her encounter in the barrow. It was undeniably strange when her colleagues talked casually about the Bronze Age woman who had lived to the age of 70 and been buried with honor, surrounded by religious trinkets and symbols. That was a very different image than that of the vulnerable young immigrant with the dead child that Lauren could recall—and quite different from the primal beauty who had given Lauren the strength to free herself from Tore, to return to herself and her own dreams.

"Maybe she liked the adventure," Lauren mused. "I'm not actually going home."

She had a job waiting near Tierradentro in Colombia. Tore had seemed either unwilling or unable to try to cross the boundaries Lauren had set to keep him away from her. Her neck had finally healed.

The road ahead seemed terrifying, wild, and cruel, but she could face that now.

AUTHOR'S NOTE

I like to take liberties, and I've taken many with the story of Egtvedpigen. If you'd like to know what the historians and archeologists really say about her, the website associated with Egtvedpigens Grav (or, in English, The Egtved Girl's Grave), the outdoor and indoor exhibition located at the mound where she was found, includes information about the find and what is known about how the girl might have lived.

If you'd like to see Egtvedpigen herself, her body is on display at the National Museum in Copenhagen. Based on chronological dating of the oak wood that made her coffin, she was buried sometime around 1370 B.C.E.

What caught my imagination was the richness of her burial – a bronze ring on each wrist, a bronze belt plate and the remains of honey-sweetened beer. Where my imagination goes once it takes off is never fully under my control. I think I expected Egtvedpigen to be the vampire at first. The story's link between the woman from the Bronze Age and Lauren Patterson, and their mutual escape from control and death, surprised me with its hopeful sense of empowerment.

• *Annabeth Leong, January 2022*

ABOUT THE AUTHOR

Annabeth Leong's writing has been recognized in a long list of best-of anthologies, including *Heiresses of Russ 2015: The Year's Best Lesbian Speculative Fiction*, *Best Women's Erotica 2015*, *Best Women's Erotica of the Year Volume 2*, *The Very Best of House of Erotica Volume One*, and several editions of *Best Lesbian Erotica*, *Best Erotic Romance*, *Best Bondage Erotica* and more.

When Circlet Press put together *Superlative Speculative Erotica: The Best of Circlet Press 2012-2017*, they asked campaign contributors to vote on which stories to include. Annabeth was the overall top vote-getter, and had the most stories make the top ten list.

Annabeth's work is always erotic, frequently speculative and often queer, though she isn't afraid to write heterosexual erotic romance set in the modern world.

Both the author and her writing can be slippery at times, drawn to exploring forbidden territory and making exquisite mistakes.

AEL Publishing recently began releasing new editions of Annabeth Leong's work, including some titles that have never before been seen.

ALSO BY ANNABETH LEONG

From AEL Publishing

Contemporary Erotic Romance Novels

Renovations

The Fugitive's Sexy Brother

Lesbian Short Fiction

If Looks Could Kink: 3 Erotic F/F Stories of Femmes on Top

www.ingramcontent.com/pod-product-compliance
Ingram Content Group UK Ltd.
Pitfield, Milton Keynes, MK11 3LW, UK
UKHW021934190726
13853UKWH00004B/1427

9 798420 991596